D0518160

NO LONGER PROPERTY
SEATTLE PUBLIC LIBRARY

All Welcome Here

by James Preller

illustrated by Mary GrandPré

FEIWEL AND FRIENDS

NEW YORK

New Stuff!

All the bright new things

Smell like sunrise, like glitter—

I am dressed, let's go!

Angelica

Like a red rocket

Flashing across a blue sky:

Her hair in the wind.

Growing Up

The old bus arrives.

Mom waves goodbye, sighs. A small

Bird flies from its nest.

A Little Scared

It's dark and noisy

and what if they aren't nice?

Someone is not sure.

Principal K.

It's his first day, too.
A dab of shaving cream, like
Snow, sits on his ear.

New Friend

This morning she clung

To her mother's knees, so scared.

Now look—a kind face!

Go down the hall, make a right,

Up the stairs, turn left,

Left, right, right,

and . . . Lost!

Directions

Harold

Like a duck, one boy

Waddles down the hall, quacking.

Yikes, he's in my class!

Name Tags

At every desk,

A chair with tennis-ball feet,

A place just for you.

OWEN

Abby

Pledge

All stand and turn to
Face the flag, hands over hearts:
Our America.

Jon-Kim

That boy can't sit still:
Impossible! Crash, boom, bang!
Fireworks splash the sky!

Class Pet

Inside his glass house,
Hamster runs in mad circles.
New hands to impress!

Exercise

We jiggle, wiggle,

Jump and stretch to tell our brains:

"Wake up! Time to think!"

Bells and Rings

The morning bells ring

Jingle-jangle in our ears.

The janitor's keys.

Hallways

A thick herd of cows

Tramples past, smelly and loud.

Fifth graders are tall.

Library

The library door
Opens: Hear the whoosh and thrum
Of the school's heart beat.

Spray!

Milk squirts out Nate's nose.

Chloe laughs and finds a friend.

A gushing firehose!

The Dessert

"You gonna eat that?"
she asks. He thinks it over,
Offers half. Yummy!

Recess

They pause, uncertain.
Really? Can we? Is it true?
Yes, recess. Run,
RUN!

I Might Say Hello

This one's long straight hair
Falls across her face; she hides
Behind black curtains.

Games

We play pirate ship.

Arrr! Scallywags walk the plank!

Brrriiinnng! Gray seas turn green.

Recess Ends

One swing still swinging.

A last pirate surrenders.

Line up, girls and boys.

Prank

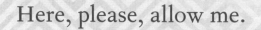
Here, please, allow me.

He smirks, twists the fountain knob.

Face splashed with laughter!

The Reading Rug

She wrestles with bears,

Travels to faraway lands.

Her nose in a book.

Shy

If she is silent

No one will know she is here.

A mouse in hiding.

Errand

"Can you deliver
this to the office?" Yes, but . . .
May I bring a friend?

Afternoon Shower

Soft rain, pitter pat.

Eyes grow heavy, lids fall low.

Windows shiver shut.

Home

At day's end, only
One question remains: "May we
come back tomorrow?"

For public school teachers everywhere, who
open their hearts and their classrooms to every
single kid who comes through that door
—J. P.

For all young artists . . . may you always
find joy in creating from your heart
—M. G.

A FEIWEL AND FRIENDS BOOK
An imprint of Macmillan Publishing Group, LLC
120 Broadway, New York, NY 10271

ALL WELCOME HERE. Text copyright © 2020 by James Preller.
Illustrations copyright © 2020 by Mary GrandPré. All rights reserved.
Printed in China by RR Donnelley Asia Printing Solutions Ltd., Dongguan City, Guangdong Province.

Our books may be purchased in bulk for promotional, educational, or business use.
Please contact your local bookseller or the Macmillan Corporate and Premium Sales Department
at (800) 221-7945 ext. 5442 or by email at MacmillanSpecialMarkets@macmillan.com.

Library of Congress Control Number: 2019948819
ISBN 978-1-250-15588-7
(hardcover)

Book design by Sophie Erb and Kathleen Breitenfeld

The art was created with acrylic paint, crayon, and oil pastel on illustration board.

Feiwel and Friends logo designed by Filomena Tuosto

First Edition, 2020

1 3 5 7 9 10 8 6 4 2

mackids.com